LUCY LOVES HORSES

BY
JAMES DAVIES

BONNEY
PRESS

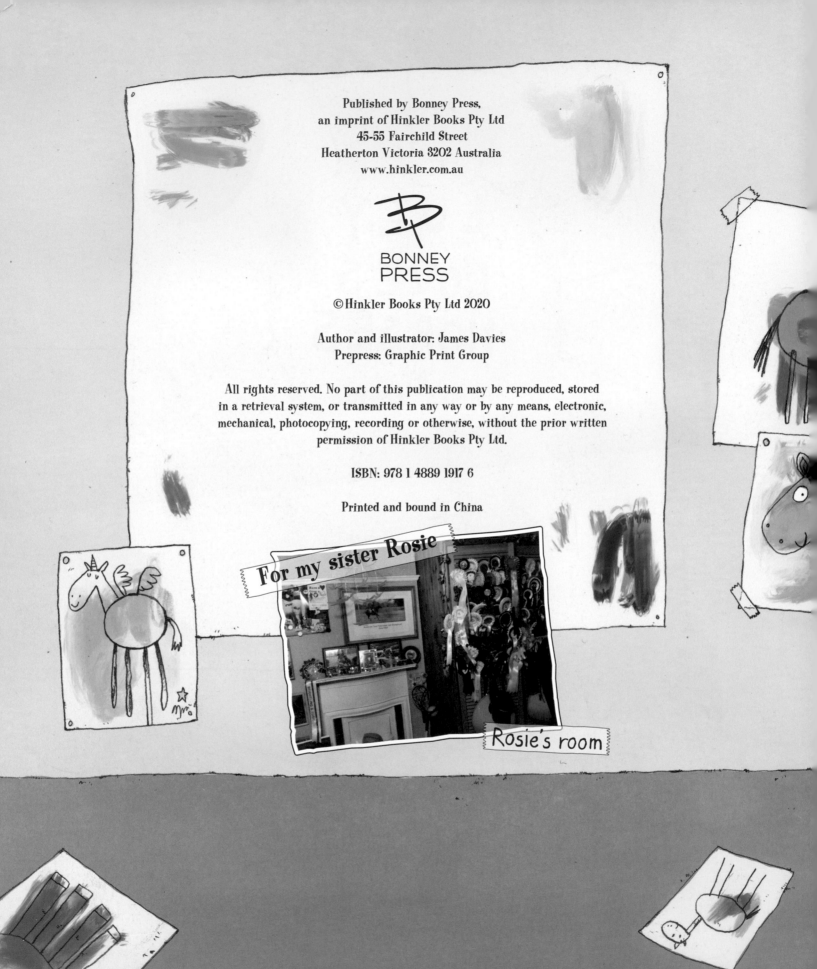

Published by Bonney Press,
an imprint of Hinkler Books Pty Ltd
45-55 Fairchild Street
Heatherton Victoria 3202 Australia
www.hinkler.com.au

BONNEY PRESS

© Hinkler Books Pty Ltd 2020

Author and illustrator: James Davies
Prepress: Graphic Print Group

ISBN: 978 1 4889 1917 6

Printed and bound in China

For my sister Rosie

Rosie's room

Lucy **loved** horses.

Not just a little...

...but a **lot**!

She had a
horse bike,

she had a horse bag,

she had  horse slippers,

 but she didn't have a **horse**.

"Muuuuuuuuuuuum..." Lucy begged. "Please, please, please can I have a horse for my birthday?"

"Let's wait and see!" said Mum.

The morning of her birthday, Lucy raced downstairs to find a big pile of presents.

"None of these look like a horse," she thought.

"We have one last present for you," said Dad, "but you have to close your eyes!"

Lucy closed her eyes as tightly as she could...

"SURPRISE!"

"What is **THAT**!?" Lucy asked.
"It's a pony!" said Mum. "Don't you like him?
His name is Hamish."

"**THAT** is not a real horse," Lucy sulked.

Lucy didn't love Hamish,

but Hamish loved Lucy.

She tried to ignore him,

but he followed her everywhere.

The next day was Lucy's birthday party.

"We have one last surprise for you," said Mum.

It was a ride on a very **big**, very **tall** horse.

"I HATE HORSES! They're too big!"

screamed Lucy.

Now, Lucy **loves** Hamish!

clip
clop
clip
clop